Dearest Kay Lynn,

We are so proud of you and your accomplishments -

We have watched you grow from a small child into a lovely young woman.

You have great leadership abilities and we know that you will continue to accomplish many worthwhile things in your life.

You are at a very important stage in your life - and there are many new adventures & experiences ahead of you -

Remember always the teachings you have had in Seminary and from all the good teachers you have had, to influence you.

Stay close to the church & teachings you know to be true. Keep your standards high, never accepting second best - for what you could have attained. If you will do this - you will always be happy!! We Love You So Very Much.

Dad and Mother

Seminary Graduation

May 20-1979

stories
of
POWER
and
PURPOSE

stories
of
POWER
and
PURPOSE

Leland E. Anderson

BOOKCRAFT INC.
SALT LAKE CITY, UTAH

Library of Congress Catalog Card Number: 74-15807

ISBN 0-88494-269-4

4th Printing, 1979

LITHOGRAPHED IN U.S.A.

PUBLISHERS PRESS
SALT LAKE CITY, UTAH

Contents

Foreword

Leland E. Anderson has a rare gift. He is a great story-teller. His experiences in many walks of life have enabled him to draw on a rich and varied career. He was born of good Scandinavian stock and grew up in Ephraim, Utah. He was a student leader in college; a principal in both public and Church schools. Later he became the superintendent of schools in two districts. He directed the seminary teacher-training program for a number of years at the Brigham Young University. He served in the U.S. Cavalry in the Mexican Border Service; filled a mission in Texas; served as a stake president; and served as principal of a seminary. He has been State Chaplain in the American Legion and District Commander in the Sixth District.

He has a keen mind and a keen memory. Like the Master Storyteller, he is gifted in seeing relationships between great principles and their practical application to daily life. This is a special gift. Even in the printed form I can hear the Danish dialect, envision the twinkle in his eyes, and see the mimicry of this great storyteller. Many a person's life will be enriched and blessed from reading these stories.

I wish my children could have Leland E. Anderson for their seminary teacher. I wish they could hear the stories I heard him tell during my four years of seminary under his excellent tutelage. It has been nearly forty years since I was a student in his classes; and yet, today, I can recall some of the stories he told—I can even remember the lessons from those stories!

We are fortunate to have the collection in this book. Many teachers will find it a rich resource with which to vitalize their lessons and make an impact on the minds and hearts of their students.

A. THEODORE TUTTLE

Home Before Chore Time

One evening as I was driving over the mountains from Nephi, Utah, to Manti, I saw a sailor in Nephi Canyon thumbing a ride. I pulled over to the side of the road and opened the door, and he got in. "Please, mister, would you let me ride with you for a little way?" he asked. "Yes, indeed I will," I said.

It seemed our conversation ended right there, because no matter how hard I tried, I could not bring him into a conversation. He just sat there and would give a little nod or a grunt to the things I was trying to talk about. Finally I gave up and quit talking.

As we reached the summit where we could look down into the Sanpete valley, with the beautiful Manti Temple in the distance, we observed that a rainstorm had just passed over the valley. And oh, what a thrill to be in the fragrance of farmland that's just been bathed in a shower.

Suddenly my companion asked me if I could stop the car, as he'd like to get out. I thought, "Well, that's all he wants from me." But he didn't get all the way out of the car — he just put one foot on the ground, kept the other in the car, and held fast to the door. Then he said, "I want to ride with you again. I just wanted to smell the air from the fields. How invigorating is the aroma of harvest time!"

I noticed his chin start to quiver somewhat, and suddenly he bowed his head and put his face in his hands. This young man, this sailor, broke down and cried like a child. When he was finally able to control himself, he said, "You don't know who you've been riding with, do you, mister?"

"No, I don't."

"Well," he said, "I'm the only child in our family. I have wonderful parents. But in my opinion, I'm one of the most worthless men who ever lived on this earth. I've been in the navy for four years, and I've had a long time to think things over. And the Lord has blessed me too, I hope.

"I lived in Mount Pleasant all my life, and I was never a very good child either. My father would call me in the morning to get up and help him with the chores, but I managed to get out of the house by a back door and go up and hide behind the stores in town. There I would work sometimes in the pool hall or the bowling alley, or do anything but the thing I should be doing."

Then with a plea in his voice, he said, "Oh, God, please, please help me that I might reach home tonight before chore time."

How many of us need to think things through in our own lives a little more carefully and say, "Help us, Father, to reach home before chore time"?

I said, "Brother, hold fast and hold tight. I'm sure we will make it."

As we drove that last seven miles to his home, the sailor was quiet, while I silently said, "Father, please help us to get there quickly, and give me the honor of meeting his parents."

As we drove up to the house, he hurried out of the car and thanked me for the ride. Then he stood on the lawn with his duffel bag. Suddenly from the kitchen door came his lovely mother and father, reaching out their arms to him and crying; and the story of the prodigal son became a reality to my own experience. The three of them stood there and wept like children, with not a word spoken.

Having had my own wish fulfilled, I felt in my heart that I had seen all I was entitled to see, so I turned the car around and drove on toward Manti.

Agency and Choice

One morning as the New Testament seminary class was about to let out, a young girl approached the teacher, William Tolman, and said, "Brother Tolman, would you like to grant me the desire of my heart?"

"If it's in righteousness, I surely would," he replied.

"Then," she said, "I want to quit this class. Give me the right to leave it. I've had all I can take."

Shocked, Brother Tolman asked, "Are you serious, Ruth?"

"Yes, I am serious."

"Well," he said, "you might consider staying in our class and auditing it. You wouldn't have to take any examinations, to hand in any papers, or to do anything but just sit and listen."

"That's a great temptation, all right, Brother Tolman. But I prefer to go."

As he walked to the door with the girl, he said, "All right, Ruth. And since I have granted you your request, will you grant me mine?"

"Yes, if I can."

"Tell me, Ruth, why do you want to quit this class?" Brother Tolman was genuinely concerned. If possible, he wanted to correct any error he had made, though he felt that he was not at fault.

The young lady looked directly at him and said, "Brother Tolman, I can't take it any longer. You have talked about free agency a number of times in class, and I have said there is no free agency — never has been and never will be. Let me give you an example. My father died when I was three years old and my mother married again. The man she married isn't worth a pinch of salt, and neither is my mother. They both drink, they both smoke, they both carouse around at night and sleep in the day. I am the servant at large. I do the work in the home. I'm promised a flogging every morning if I don't get home in a hurry to fix dinner for them and to clean the house.

"When I went to high school last fall the principal told me that the class of which I was a member had to take seminary at this particular time. There was no other place to go. So I didn't have my free agency there either. I came and took the class because I was invited to, there was nothing else to do. Now, for once in my life, I would like to establish free agency as an active principle in my faith. The first thing I want is to be free of this class."

Brother Tolman was silent for a moment. Then he said: "Ruth, I've enjoyed you in this class very much   And I want you to know, if you ever change your mind and want to come back to this class, no matter what day of the week it is, remember that when you walk through that door you will make me the happiest man in the seminary system."

About two weeks later Ruth came back. She sat on a back seat in the class and didn't take any kind of part in the class discussion. After class she came up to Brother Tolman and said, "I'd like to come back and identify with the class, if you will let me."

"Oh, Ruth, will I let you! Welcome, a thousand times, welcome!"

"The only reason I'm doing this is because I want to. It's an exercise of my free agency," she added.

"Ah, that's fine," he replied.

The next day after class she asked Brother Tolman,

"Would it be possible for me to have a seat right near the front? I want to get everything that's said in class."

"Yes," he said, "tomorrow I will let you change seats with anyone you may choose."

That week Brother Tolman told the class their journals would be due on Friday. After class Ruth told him, "Brother Tolman, may I hand in my journal too? I have been keeping it up all the time I was away, and for only one reason — that was because I wanted to."

"Oh, by all means, hand it in, Ruth."

On Friday Ruth handed in a lovely journal. Brother Tolman announced in class that day that there would be a test the following Wednesday. After class Ruth asked him, "Brother Tolman, may I take the test? I am prepared for it. I have been keeping up with my lessons right along — because I wanted to."

And this pleased him very much.

The next week Ruth again came to him after class one day and said, "Brother Tolman, from now on you may call on me to pray any morning in this class that you want to, because I have been doing some earnest soul-searching since I left, and on my knees I have been constantly asking God to help me in this great work."

Ruth had learned and seemed to fully appreciate that great truth: that liberty without law is an utterly impossible experience.

Don't Dam Your Spiritual Garden

"Love your enemies, bless them that curse you, do good to them that hate you, and pray for them which despitefully use you, and persecute you." (Matthew 5:44.)

This is an important teaching from the Savior's Sermon on the Mount. That Sermon also states, "Blessed are they which are persecuted for righteousness' sake: for theirs is the kingdom of heaven." (Matthew 5:10.) A saintly life invites one to pray for his enemies.

A wonderful Sunday School teacher once inspired my classmates and me, almost "stabbed" us all wide awake as would a divine surgeon, with the necessity of living daily in a manner pleasing to the Lord. He made us feel that our sacred scriptures could always be a point of reference that would lead us to God's celestial kingdom. A powerful testimony of this came to me as a result of an experience in my daily life, an experience that was truly a crossroads to me.

In my home town was a large pea factory. Peas were never picked in the patch; they were cut in the vine like hay, and loaded — green vines and all — on a hay wagon. A relatively small forkful could seem like a load of lead.

One morning as I was mowing some alfalfa, the fieldman from the factory came to me and said, "Your pea patch is ready right now to be harvested." This is a crucial point — a few hours of too much sunshine turns peas in a pod from first-class to hard tack. Much value of the crop is lost if it is not cut on time.

I moved my team and hay-cutting equipment to the five-acre pea patch and in a short time had cut all the hayrack would hold; in fact, it was all my small team could pull. With some effort and the help of a switch, I managed to get the team to pull the load to the hardened field road. Then we proceeded toward the factory a mile away. However, I had forgotten all about the old field ditch, full of water, which my team had to cross. Would I ever make it?

I soon discovered the answer. Approaching the ditch, I first gave the team a much-needed rest. Then, with positive urging, they shot across the ditch — but the front wheels hit the mud and sank up to the hub!

The only solution was for me to unload all the peas on the ground, pull the empty wagon across, and then proceed to carry the peas and replace them upon the wagon. The very thought made me tired. If only another team and wagon would appear on the scene — maybe two teams could pull me out!

Then up the road I could see an outfit coming in my direction. Help was in sight. As the wagon came closer, however, my heart sank. It was my neighbor who lived down the road and who did not help anyone. He didn't have to — he was rich in worldly goods.

As he pulled up beside me, he stopped his outfit and smilingly said, "So, you're stuck, are you, Lee?" I was surprised he knew my name. He had never talked to me before. I replied that my load was too big for my small team. His smile grew larger as he said, "Well, good luck to you," and away he went down the lane.

Never was I so angry! What I called him cannot be printed — I even spoke in Danish so my team couldn't understand! For the moment I reappraised the law of Moses. I looked up into the sky and said, "Oh, Father, give me the chance to meet him on the desert sometime, choking for a good drink of water. Let me have a barrel of water in my truck so I can pour it out onto the sand and tell him to scratch."

Somehow I managed to get to the factory. I succeeded in getting all of my peas harvested in time, and though my feelings were still on edge they had mellowed somewhat.

Evil seldom requires a down payment; it's like installment buying. My hope — and my day — finally arrived. A few days later, while proceeding to my farm, as I approached this roadblock to my farming efforts, the ditch, I nearly choked with happiness. I found my unobliging neighbor stuck in the same ditch with a load of peas!

Before I reached the scene of trouble, like a bolt of lightning my Sunday School teacher's lesson on retaliation came to my mind. I tried to unload the thought, but it was deeply entrenched in my soul. Our Savior said, "And whosoever shall compel thee to go a mile, go with him twain." (Matthew 5:41.) Now or never was my life to be molded by love or hatred. The Lord had said, "Agree with thine adversary quickly, whiles thou art in the way with him." (Matthew 5:25.) I did! I kicked the adversary off the wagon.

As I pulled up beside my brother, I stopped and repeated to him his own words: "So you're stuck, are you, brother?" I hoped he would learn from this new experience the lesson that Cain learned in the garden, that there is no such thing as liberty without law.

My neighbor responded that he could not proceed without help. I did not wait longer. I jumped off my wagon, took from it a long chain, and secured it properly onto the end of his wagon tongue. Then the two teams put their shoulders to the wheel and in short order they were all standing on dry ground.

In deep embarrassment, my neighbor said, "Thanks, Lee. I appreciate your kindness." Then he added, "How much do I owe you?"

My reply was not altogether honest. "I enjoyed helping you out of that ditch," I said.

We both went on our way rejoicing. I could hardly hold my team — they seemed to want to trot. And I caught myself whistling and singing "Come, Come Ye Saints."

A couple of days later I found a new bridge over the ditch. I smiled as I learned who had obliged all the north field farmers with this needed contribution.

Two weeks later, while cutting more hay one day, I noticed a man coming down through my field. It was my neighbor. "Let your team have a break, while we settle the problems of the world," he said. So we visited for a few minutes. Then, as he started to leave, he looked squarely at me and, in halting phrases, apologized for leaving me in the ditch.

I have often wondered just which one of us was the unneighborly one. When had I ever volunteered to him any kindness? The injured one may well be the one at times who seeks confrontation and better understanding. We both learned a valuable lesson that day.

About His Father's Business

In the New Testament we read of Jesus as a boy, twelve years of age, speaking with the lawyers and doctors in the temple. They were astonished at his understanding and answers. Mary and Joseph too were amazed. When they asked him why he had dealt with them in such a manner, he replied, " . . . wist ye not that I must be about my Father's business?" (Luke 2:49.)

A forceful application of this event was related to me by my uncle, Joseph Johansen, from Mount Pleasant, Utah. He served in the mission field in Washington and Oregon, when Elder Melvin J. Ballard of the Council of the Twelve was president of that mission. This is his story as he related it to me:

"One day I received a telegram from Elder Ballard to meet him at a certain station in a small town. There was pressing business to take care of in that part of the Lord's vineyard, and he wanted me with him. I went down to the depot on the appointed day, and as I sat waiting for the train to come in, the depot agent approached me and said: 'Why are you sitting here? Who are you waiting for?'

"I replied, 'I am waiting for the passenger train to pull in, because I am to meet a certain man who is on that train.'

" 'Well,' said the agent, 'then you may go home. This train is a through train, and under no condition will it ever stop at this station.'

" 'If you don't mind, will you pardon me if I sit here and watch the train go through town?' I replied.

" 'You may do so — that is your right,' the agent said."

On the train that day Elder Ballard asked the conductor if he would please stop the train at that particular station and let him off, because he had a very important meeting to hold. The conductor smiled and said, "You bet I will not stop this train. This is a through train. If I should stop it there, I might be the cause of a serious wreck. And besides, even if I didn't have a wreck, I would be fired from my job, because this train does not stop at that station." Elder Ballard thanked him as he continued on through the train.

Well, instead of going nonstop through the station, the train pulled onto the siding and stopped. For the first time in forty years, a too-lengthy freight train had pulled into the town half an hour before the passenger train was due. When it pulled onto the siding to let the passenger train pass, it proved to be too long for the siding.

Since the freight train could not be pulled off the main track, it backed up on the main track and waited for the passenger train to come in. Then the passenger train had to take the siding and wait while the freight train passed on through the town. During this time the conductor sought out Elder Ballard and said, "Mister, this has never happened before in forty years. May I ask, Who are you?"

Elder Ballard gave an answer similar to that of the Savior in the temple: "I am a minister of the gospel and I am about my Father's business. I knew this train would stop. I had faith that it would."

Confirmation that he was indeed on his Father's business came later that evening. Elder Ballard and the missionaries went out to an Indian reservation, where they spoke. As the apostle was speaking, the Indian chief came up from the audience, threw his arms around him, and said to his people: "This is the man I told you about that I saw in my dream. He has a book that purports to be the history of our people. Give heed to his teachings and counsel this night."

Single-Direction Salvation

Once a father and his son were driving in a buggy going east through Spanish Fork Canyon in Utah. As they drove along, they met a long freight train speeding west through the canyon. The son was intrigued by what he saw: a man running along the tops of the cars eastward, toward the end of the train.

"Do you see what I see?" asked the young man.

"And what do you see, my boy?"

"I see a man running along the train, going in the opposite direction from the train. The other night in our home evening discussion you said that no man can go in two directions at the same time. What I see now destroys the truthfulness of your statement."

The father thought for a moment, then asked, "And if the man keeps on running, what is sure to happen to him?"

"He will be thrown off," said the boy, beginning to see the true picture of what was happening.

"Yes," replied the wise father. "That is what the Church is like. It is moving on in its program of salvation, bringing to pass the immortality and eternal life of man. Whenever we cease to do things with an eye single to the glory of God, our fall-off is certain."

The Worth of a Soul

In one of my classrooms at Brigham Young University there hung a picture of Jesus Christ, our Lord and Savior — a painting so real, so much like the Son of God as I envisioned him, that I studied it many times and read many things into it.

One day I became very personal and said aloud, "Lord, how much am I worth?" I did not receive an answer then, but one evening while I was reading the first chapter in the Pearl of Great Price it was revealed to me: "For behold, this is my work and my glory — to bring to pass the immortality and eternal life of man." (Moses 1:39.) In the Gospel of Luke it becomes a revealed personal touch: "Simon, Simon, behold, Satan hath desired to have you, that he may sift you as wheat: But I have prayed for thee, that thy faith fail not: and when thou art converted, strengthen thy brethren." (Luke 22:31-32.)

In 1938 at a stake quarterly conference in Ephraim, Utah, Elder Charles A. Callis told a forceful story that made a strong impression on me as well as others who heard it.

Elder Callis had been born in Dublin, Ireland, of poverty-stricken parents. At the age of eight he was baptized into The Church of Jesus Christ of Latter-day Saints. Shortly thereafter he attended a branch meeting and heard a missionary give his farewell talk before returning to his home in Wyoming. In his talk the missionary said his mission had been a failure because he had baptized but one person — and that a ragged little boy.

A few years later the Callis family emigrated to America, where they struggled hard to make a living, and Charles had to work in a coal mine. Then he was called to the Southern States Mission, and his two years' service there revealed the strength of this son of God. He was made mission president and served in that capacity for more than twenty-five years. Later he was ordained an apostle.

One of his first conference assignments as a General Authority was to a stake in Wyoming. There he searched for the missionary who had baptized him in Great Britain — and who had called himself a failure. He succeeded in finding the missionary, and they spent a rich evening together.

In the course of their visit Elder Callis asked the man, "Elder, do you remember the last sermon you gave as a British missionary, when you claimed failure because you had baptized just one ragged little boy?"

"Yes," the elder said, "and I have often wondered what became of him."

Elder Callis smiled and said, "I am that boy."

In a poem quoted often by Elder Adam S. Bennion we find a beautiful benediction to this experience:

> *Perchance in heaven one day to me*
> *Some blessed Saint shall come and say,*
> *"All hail, beloved, but for thee,*
> *My soul to death had fallen prey."*
> *And oh, what rapture in the thought,*
> *One soul to glory to have brought!*

We Need Never Be Alone

One day I asked the students in my seminary class, "What would you do if you should wake one morning and discover during the night every person on earth had passed away?"

One boy raised his hand and almost shouted, "I would go downtown and rob the bank," which drew broad smiles from others in the class.

I have thought a great deal about his answer. From whom would he rob? What would be the value of the money in his hands? Did it have any exchange value? Can anyone sin unto himself alone? Can a man rob himself? Can a man rob God?

I doubt that any man can live unto himself alone. Countless words have been written on relationships that should exist in the home between parents and their children, particularly between mother and daughter, father and son.

In the rush of time, life sometimes seems to find us a slave to the clock and the social timetable, and our home duties all too often are neglected. The impact of this came to me forcefully once when a long-promised deer hunt with my only son finally came to pass.

Oh, what fun we had planning that trip! And how glorious when the day finally arrived! Our cabin high up Manti Canyon was the place from which we set out — a forty-five-year-old man and his sixteen-year-old son. Little did I dream the difference that his strength would make in twelve inches of snow and the lesson we both would learn that day.

As we moved together through the spruce tamaracks, I gradually slowed down, but not my son. I motioned to him to hold up a moment while I caught my breath. Also, we were about on dead center of heavy deer activity, and I knew that one should never walk away from home base to the point of exhaustion. There is always a return journey to be faced.

My son then suggested that we circle back to camp. Never have we been so united on a plan! He suggested that he carry my gun too — to which I tried to smile, but my face was frozen. As we entered a hollow area, I found his arm around my waist, giving me welcome assistance. Then he smiled at me and confessed that this was the greatest hunt of his life. "Just think, Dad," he said, "what a thrill this has been for both of us! Not a gun fired, and no other hunter seen or heard from."

The quietness of the forest did seem awesome, and my son said that to be there, in the solitude, just the two of us, was a sacred experience to him.

To me, our experience was not exactly the same as he had described it, and I searched for words to express my feelings. "My boy," I began, "we are not alone. We have not been alone all day."

"But I have seen no one, nor have I heard a shot on this hunt," he said.

Then I reassured him that in my prayers the night before I had prayed that we might have just such an experience — that the Lord would walk beside us and keep us from harm and evil. "I have felt his presence," I said, "and in you, I have envisioned eternity."

"Thanks, Dad," my son replied. "I hope I shall ever cherish this lesson."

In the organization of this world, when he placed his children upon it, the Lord said, "It is not good for man to be alone." The law of eternal marriage was given to enforce this truth. The great preacher in Ecclesiastes observed, ". . . but woe to him that is alone when he falleth; for he hath not another to help him up." (Ecclesiastes 4:10.)

Because he had greater physical strength, my son carried my gun; but he learned that there was another greater than he. We were not alone. Jesus himself was never alone. He declared that his Father was ever with him. May he always be with and abide with each of us.

"A Form of Godliness"

In the mission field many years ago I learned a lesson that helped me to understand better the Lord's response when Joseph Smith, in the First Vision, asked which of all the sects was right. He was told that he should join none of them, that their creeds were an abomination in the Lord's sight; that "they draw near to me with their lips, but their hearts are far from me, they teach for doctrines the commandments of men, having a form of godliness, but they deny the power thereof." (See Joseph Smith 2:18-19.)

As I was tracting in Dallas, Texas, I knocked at the door of a home. The woman who answered the door, when told who I was, said, "I'm sorry, but we have been instructed by our fathers not to entertain ministers of any other faith. Our ministers are the head of the church, and from them we shall receive our doctrine and our religion. And I am well satisfied with my faith."

I told her that I admired her for being loyal to her church, but that on this particular morning I was feeling lonesome, in an area far from my home. Wouldn't she just be willing to share with me a few thoughts of godliness?

After thinking it over a moment, she said, "Well, I'll tell you what I will do. I'll tell you about the most glorious experience I ever had in my life, if you promise not to interrupt."

I assured her that I would respect her wishes and would listen, adding with a smile, "That's sort of a woman's right and prerogative — so you go right ahead and I'll be a good listener."

"Well," she began, "this past summer I was baptized in the Jordan River. You'll never know what a marvelous experience that was — the greatest experience of my life."

Though I had promised not to interrupt, I couldn't help exclaiming, "Oh, how I would like to have an experience like that! If I were ever baptized in the Jordan River, I would feel that maybe this is where John the Baptist took Jesus down into the river and baptized him. I am sure that this would be a glorious experience long to be remembered."

"Oh," she remarked, "I have never been to Palestine."

"Then you have lost me somewhere along the way," I replied. "What did you mean?"

"Well, you see, my priest was over to the Holy Land this past summer, and while there he got a gallon jug and filled it with water from the Jordan River. And just recently some of us in the church here were highly favored by coming into his private room, where he sprinkled us with water from the Jordan River. I will always think of that as my baptismal day, and what a glorious experience it was!"

I paused, then said, "Oh, please forgive me. I promised not to interrupt, but I must tell you about the glorious experience I had. I too have been baptized, in one of the temples of our God, in Manti, Utah. There, a high priest of God took me into the waters of baptism, and after repeating these lines — 'Brother Leland E. Anderson, having been commissioned of Jesus Christ, I baptize you in the name of the Father, and of the Son, and of the Holy Ghost'— he immersed me in the water. And as I came forth up out of the water, I hope it was as a new man. This baptism is a glorious experience, one that I should like to share with you. I know I promised not to interrupt you, but I just wanted to rejoice with you in the experience I also have had in being baptized."

She immediately refused my offer of literature on the subject of baptism and said that her priest would keep her well informed. "I've kept my promise," she said, "and told you about my baptism. And now, to be a faithful Catholic, I must say good morning to you."

As she closed the door, she left me wondering how the Spirit of truth would ever penetrate her soul. This experience has remained vivid in my mind ever since, reminding me how beautifully the Father portrayed the feelings of so many otherwise fine people: "They draw near to me with their lips, but their hearts are far from me; they teach for doctrines the commandments of men, having a form of godliness, but they deny the power thereof."

"Prepare to Follow Me"

All my life I have been taught that it is the set of the sail that determines the way we shall go. Several years ago my wife and I were in an air terminal near Boston with twelve hours to wait until our plane would take off. We purchased a number of postcards illustrating the history of Boston in photos of yesteryear.

Since my major field of study was American history, I was intensely interested in the cards. And since time lay heavy on our hands, I suggested that we learn even more about the local history by visiting a cemetery.

As we moved among the headstones at the cemetery, reading the inscriptions, I was intrigued by one that seemed to give us a message from above as well as from below. The inscription read:

> *Friend, as you are now, so once was I.*
> *As I am now, you soon will be.*
> *So, friend, prepare to follow me.*

Someone had completed the inscription by writing with a piece of chalk this addendum:

> *To follow you I'll not consent*
> *Until I know which way you went.*

To me, this illustrates the thinking of youth today. They demand to know why and when and where. Theirs is a questioning attitude. They wish to be shown a better way, well documented by religion and science. This, then, makes them all potentially choice, for they came not long since from the presence of our Father.

"A Little Child Shall Lead Them"

One beautiful February morning a number of years ago, as I left the drugstore in Manti for my office, I noticed in the window a large picture of George Washington. Two first-grade boys were looking at it, and I stopped to listen to their conversation.

One boy, after looking for some time, finally said, "Gee, isn't he a great guy! I sure love him. You know, he's the father of our country. He's the man who's holding us together. We talk so much about him in school that I feel sometimes as if he is really there."

The other boy listened, then turned to him and said, "Say, listen. Don't you know George Washington is dead?"

Shocked, the first boy asked, "When did he die?"

"Why, he's been dead for many years."

"Well," replied the young lad, "he isn't dead in my life. I think he's very much alive."

In a similar vein, at one of my classes at Brigham Young University, a student who was training to be a seminary teacher told us that one day, while driving from his home state of Oregon to Utah, he noticed a sign by the side of the road. I don't remember the exact words, but it said, in essence, "Come on, America. Wake up! There is no God. Religion is just an opiate to keep us happy and ignorant."

The student, in relating this incident, said, "Well, that was a terrible thing, and it made me angry. I was about to go back and tear the sign down but just then I noticed another sign, about four feet wide and perhaps two hundred yards long, tacked up on the turn of the road. It said, 'I'm sorry, mister, that your God is dead. I want you to know that my God is very much alive and is a visitor in our home often.' "

As I've thought about this experience, in my own mind I've concluded that the two signs weren't much different from the two signs in the boys' hearts as they stood looking at the picture in the drugstore window. To the one, George Washington was very much alive; to the other, he was dead.

One person has said that what the world needs today is a divine surgeon to stab us wide awake to the many blessings of our Father and the wonderful opportunities we have. And with these blessings and opportunities go something that's highly incumbent on us all: to match them with good citizenship.

We need faith — a living faith. And what is faith? From some young children we get these answers: "Faith is like a farmer. He plants his seed knowing it will grow." "Faith is like a searchlight. Its ever-forward beam lights the way for safe travel." "Faith gives assurance of a safe voyage." "Faith is like love — it cannot be forced." "Faith is like electricity. It cannot be seen, but it is felt." "Faith is like yeast. It gives growth beyond innate ability." Yes, faith is all these and more. May each of us have faith in a Supreme Being who watches over and loves and guides us in all our actions.

Preaching to Spirits in Prison

While I was serving in the mission field in Dallas, Texas, my companion, Elder Cleon Payne, and I were called to go into the state penitentiary each Thursday to preach to the inmates there. Each week we went into the cellblocks and spoke to eight different groups of people, and sometimes we would sing to them and they to us.

One day we were taken to a private room where about fifty women prisoners were gathered. As we looked around the group, we felt that perhaps the prison officials had made a mistake in allowing us to be at liberty in the same room with these women, because of the mean, hateful looks they gave us. We were both scared. Elder Payne whispered to me, "What on earth shall we do?"

"Let's sing a song," I suggested.

He thought that was a pretty good idea and asked what we should sing. I prayed silently to the Lord for guidance and then said, "Let's sing 'Love at Home.' "

Now that's quite a song to sing in a penitentiary, where the surroundings are anything but home. But we did our best, and as we finished the first verse, we saw that about half the women in the room were crying. By the time we finished the second verse, just about everyone was crying, including Elder Payne and myself.

Then, through the inspiration of the Lord, we spoke to them the best we knew how. At the close of the meeting one lady stood up and said, "May we shake hands with you?"

Of course we agreed, and the women came up one by one to shake our hands.

The last girl to pass through the line appeared to be about nineteen years of age. I said to her, "Sister, may I ask you a very personal question?"

She said, in the prison vernacular, "Shoot!"

I said, "What on earth did a lovely girl like you ever do in your life to get in a place like this?"

She looked right at us and answered, "The reason for my being here is found in the answer to your song, 'Love at Home.' I am here because there was no love in our home."

As I've thought about that experience through the years, I've thought how much it was like the experience of the Savior, whose great message was one of love, and who, according to Peter, "also hath once suffered for sins, the just for the unjust, that he might bring us to God, being put to death in the flesh, but quickened by the Spirit: by which also he went and preached unto the spirits in prison." (1 Peter 3:18-19.)

When Jesus first took upon himself his missionary labors in his home town of Nazareth, he stood up and said to the people: "The Spirit of the Lord is upon me, because he hath anointed me to preach the gospel to the poor; he hath sent me to heal the brokenhearted, to preach deliverance to the captives, and recovering of sight to the blind, to set at liberty them that are bruised." (Luke 4:18.)

How incumbent it is upon each of us to do the best we can to create love among people — in our own homes, in our places of business, in all our relationships! The Savior informed us that the first great laws of life were (1) to love God, (2) to love our neighbor, and (3) to love ourselves. With our lives based upon love, we cannot go wrong.

How Many Is One?

A fine seminary teacher told me the following memorable story:

One morning the principal of the high school adjacent to where he taught seminary called him and said he had a senior boy who was a problem to every teacher. He had been promoted each year probably because his teachers thought the day would come when they would be rid of him.

Every Monday morning he came to school under the influence of liquor. He caroused around and smoked and had the strong spirit of immorality in his soul.

"John," the principal said, "this boy, Jack, is in my office now. He has given us much trouble, and I told him that the only thing that will save his neck is the promise from him that he will go over to your seminary and take a class in Church history with you."

The seminary teacher thought, "What on earth did I ever do to inherit this?"

"Well," the principal said, "he is on his way over to see you now, and I expect you to carry on from this morning."

The teacher had the class seated in the form of a big U, around his desk, and as Jack came ambling in through a door at the rear the teacher said to him, "Brother Jack, will you please come up and sit in the left front here?"

Jack replied, in a surly way, "I'll sit wherever I please," and he walked right through the class up to the right front and sat down.

The teacher hardly knew what to do. He took hold of the desk with both hands and held tight, then silently whispered to the Lord, "Who is going to save face, this big lunk or me?" And the answer came to him, "You are not employed to save *your* face; you are employed to save *his* face." With that, the teacher took over.

In the days that followed he exercised all the patience and love and perseverance he could with the young man. He also pleaded with the class to treat Jack like a brother. And by the end of the school year the boy was one of the best students in the class. He had stopped smoking and drinking, and for the first time in his life he could take a girl out on a date without any ulterior motive.

Jack took an important part in the class graduation exercises that year and received a diploma. Then he was drafted into the U.S. Army and sent to a base in California for his basic training. While in California he became a good friend of a young Protestant. They lived in the same barracks and spent much of their free time together. Jack invited the friend to attend Church services with him many times, but he refused to do so until near the end of the summer, when he agreed to attend a sacrament meeting with Jack.

One afternoon that fall a young serviceman knocked at the door of the seminary teacher's office. He was invited in, and as they sat down to chat, the serviceman told the teacher of a great spiritual experience he had had that he just could not forget.

He said that he had finally consented, on the last day he was in camp, to go to the Latter-day Saint services with Jack. "It was one of those meetings where each person was at liberty to stand up and tell how good the Lord had been to him and his family," he said, apparently referring to a fast and testimony meeting.

"As I sat in the middle of that big audience with Jack — there must have been several hundred persons there that day

— Jack finally stood up and started to bear his testimony. And I was never so frightened in my life, because everyone turned and looked, and I felt that they were looking at me and wondering who I was.

"Then Jack left me sitting there all alone while he walked up to the front and stood at the microphone. 'I want to look into the faces of you people while I bear my testimony,' he said. 'I am most grateful to the Lord this day for a man who has indeed been a savior to me — a man who picked me up when I was down and who taught me the gospel of Jesus Christ in all its beauty. That man was my seminary teacher.' It wasn't long until practically everyone in that congregation was crying," the serviceman continued, "and I, a Protestant, sat there and cried too.

"Now Jack didn't ask me to come and tell you this. He doesn't know that I'm in your office now. But I want you to know that you have been a savior to that boy, for he has incorporated into his behavior, patterns of living of what I suppose would be considered a good Mormon boy."

A few weeks went by, and then one evening, just before Christmas, the seminary teacher knocked on my door. As I opened it, there he stood with a young man in uniform. It was the same boy who previously had visited him in his office. The teacher said, "Brother Anderson, I want you to meet this young man. He's the one who's been living with Jack. He is deeply concerned about the gospel and wants to know more about it."

Now I ask, How many is one? Jack will probably one day be married in the proper place and will become a parent in Israel. His beloved friend too by this time has in all probability become a member of the Church. What can we do, what may we do, to inspire those who need us? The challenge is before us, and I ask God to inspire us that we might follow him and do everything with an eye single to his glory.

Tomorrow May Be Too Late

Since the days of Father Adam, the Lord has taught mankind to accept Him as their Savior and to walk in His path. Herein will man find happiness. Alma beautifully proclaims: "For behold, this life is the time for men to prepare to meet God; yea, behold the day of this life is the day for men to perform their labors." (Alma 34:32.)

He also states: "Ye cannot say, when ye are brought to that awful crisis, that I will repent, that I will return to my God. Nay, ye cannot say this; for that same spirit which doth possess your bodies at the time that ye go out of this life, that same spirit will have power to possess your body in that eternal world." (Alma 34:34.)

In the framework of these scriptures, I recall an experience a seminary teacher told of a lawyer who had finished his studies in law and returned to the rural community he had been raised in. Wondering what to do and how to organize and set up law practice became his great concern.

Early one morning he was walking up through the main street of his home town to see if any new buildings had gone up in his absence. About the time the sun was coming up, he looked down the road and saw a horse hitched to a buggy coming down the road toward him as fast as the horse could run. In the parlance of that community, that was a good old-fashioned runaway.

The lawyer dashed out into the road and, as the animal ran swiftly past him, grabbed the horse by the bit with one hand and by the hame of the harness with the other. He was dragged for some distance but finally succeeded in getting his footing and stopping the horse. He then led the animal over to a tree and tied him up.

As he peeked into the buggy to see if there was anyone in it, he saw a sweet little baby boy in a bassinette. About that time two very excited parents rode up in another buggy, jumped out, and came running up, crying, "Oh, how is our baby?"

The lawyer answered that the baby had apparently enjoyed the ride and had been left none the worse for it. The parents thanked him and rode off with their child.

Twenty years passed. The lawyer had become a judge in one of the districts of the state. One day a young man accused of murder was brought before him. When the trial was over, the jury returned a verdict of murder in the first degree. On the day appointed for sentencing, the judge said to the young man: "I hereby sentence you to the state penitentiary where you will be shot and your life taken from you for committing this act. Now, my young man, have you any final statements that you would like to make?"

The boy smiled and said, "Judge, about twenty years ago early one morning, do you remember stopping a runaway horse in your home town and saving a baby's life?"

"Yes," replied the judge. "I recall that day. I've often wondered what happened to that boy."

"That boy is the one you have just sentenced to death," was the answer. "It's an interesting thing, Judge. Years ago you saved my life; today you are taking it."

The judge paused a moment to reflect, then said: "You see, son, yesterday I was your savior; today I am your judge."

Sometimes tomorrow is too late. If a man does not accept the Savior in this life as his Lord and keep His commandments, of a surety he will have to face the inevitable judgment in the next life when the books are opened, and he will be judged by those things he has done.

The Sorrow of Being Rejected

In the Christmas season of 1924 I was attending the University of Utah, and my wife and I were both doing all we could to make financial ends meet. We didn't have any money for Christmas presents that year, but we enjoyed sharing with each other the beautiful story of the nativity found in the scriptures.

One evening about two days before Christmas I suggested that we go downtown to look at the beautiful displays in the windows of the shops; it wouldn't cost us a cent, and we often had a lot of fun doing this.

At about 11:00 P.M. we were in front of a jewelry shop, admiring the glittering displays of diamond rings, watches, and bracelets. I pointed out to my wife some of the beautiful items and said, pointing to a certain ring, "Do you see that, sweetheart? Someday I'll buy you one like that — in fact, I'll buy you all the jewelry you can hold." I didn't notice that while I was speaking, she had moved to the next window, and that another lady had come up alongside me and was admiring the jewelry. Still looking at the displays, I put my arm around the woman and said, "Yes, sir, sweetheart, someday I'll buy you plenty of this."

That's as far as I got, for I suddenly found myself dodging some ferocious jabs from this woman. "Pardon me," I exclaimed. "I'm sorry about this. I thought you were my wife." And in an excited voice she said, "Yes, I've heard that story before, too!"

About that time a policeman walked by, and the woman ran up to him and said, "Officer, this man is annoying me."

The officer came over to me and asked, "Well now, my boy, just what have you got to say to that?"

I answered; "Officer, I guess in a way she's right, but in a bigger way she's wrong. You see, my wife and I are going to school and we didn't have money to buy Christmas presents, so we thought we'd do some window shopping. And I thought this woman was my wife standing by my side when I accidentally put my arm around her and told her of the Christmas presents I would get her someday."

"Yes, I've heard that story before, too," the officer said. Then he added, "Tell me, where is your wife? I don't see her."

Looking around, I said, "You just look over there by that next window. That's my wife."

About that time my wife turned and looked straight at us, with a broad smile. The officer took me by the arm and walked over to her and said, "Lady, is this your husband?"

And she answered, "Officer, I have never seen him in my life before."

"Well," the officer declared, "I caught you in two lies. didn't I? Why don't you come along with me!"

He started to pull me down the street, but that's as far as my wife could laugh it off. She ran up to him and said, "Oh, Officer, I just had to get some good joke on him — he's always pulling so many fast ones on me. He really is my husband. He didn't know I'd left that window and gone over to the next one. This lady walked up by his side, and he still thought it was me."

Well, it was Christmastime, and we all saw the humor in the situation, so we had a good hearty laugh, wished each other a merry Christmas, and went on our way.

In my life on different occasions I've heard of men who have lost a lovely wife in death and who, up to that time, had been fine Christian men. Then, in sorrow and loneliness, they have reverted to bad habits and forfeited the blessings of the priesthood and temple marriage.

When such a man has died, I've been told, he has found his wife all right, but as she has looked at him she has said, "I'm sorry, but I don't know you. Under no condition will I ever carry on from here and through eternity with you as my husband."

What sorrow! What a terrible thing to be rejected in the hereafter! Now I haven't died yet, but if I'm rejected in the next world by my loved ones, I don't believe I could feel any worse than I did for a few moments that lovely Christmas Eve in Salt Lake City.

"Except the Lord Build the House"

"Except the Lord build the house, they labour in vain that build it. . . . " (Psalm 127:1.) What house?

For several years my wife and I were ordinance workers in the Manti Temple, and we seldom missed the opportunity of going into the sealing room to watch young people be sealed to each other for time and eternity.

One day a particularly fine young couple went through the temple, then knelt at the altar to be sealed. The sealing ordinance was of divine authorship, and it brought tears to the eyes of both of them. When they were pronounced man and wife and their marriage was sealed by a kiss and also by the Holy Spirit of promise, they walked out of the room arm in arm as one.

It so happened that that day as we left the temple, just in front of us was this lovely young couple who had just been married. The husband, oblivious to all that was going on about him, stopped once more and put his arms around his bride and gave her a resounding kiss. Then he said, "Sweetheart, I'm going to work hard, and we're going to have all the blessings of the earth. I'll build you a mansion to live in and I will dress you in furs and silks and satins."

My wife looked into my eyes and whispered, "You never promised me anything like that."

"No, I didn't," I replied. "But let me tell you — you and I are very rich people. Of course we don't have much money. But we have something for which we should be truly thankful — six lovely children and the wonderful feeling that the gospel net will preserve us, through faithfulness, into a glorious hereafter."

Well, I couldn't help but go up and wish this couple well and give them a send-off for the new world into which they had just entered. I said, "Brother, if you don't object, I'd like to respond to what we just overheard you promise your wife. Let me ask you to read something you will find in the book of Psalms, wherein David says, 'Except the Lord build the house, they labour in vain that build it.' We give you this thought from both of us and wish you Godspeed and a world of future happiness."

May each of us remember the words of the Lord:

" . . . Ye are the temple of the living God; as God hath said, I will dwell in them, and walk in them; and I will be their God, and they shall be my people." (2 Corinthians 6-16.)

" . . . Know ye not that your body is the temple of the Holy Ghost which is in you, which ye have of God, and ye are not your own? . . . therefore glorify God in your body, and in your spirit, which are God's." (1 Corinthians 6:19-20.)

" . . . He that cometh to God must believe that he is, and that he is a rewarder of them that diligently seek him." (Hebrews 11:6.)

What house? The Lord's, of course.

Parental Surrender to Love

A stake president in northern Utah once asked me to come and speak to the youth of his stake. The stake leaders were doing everything in their power to give the youth new hope, new faith, new life and endeavor in the forces of love.

As we sat upon the stand and viewed some nine hundred young people between the ages of twelve and twenty-one (no parents were invited), all sons and daughters of God and not long away from his presence, the stake president leaned over to me and said, "Brother Anderson, I've never been so frightened in my life."

"Why are you afraid?" I asked.

"Well, after you finish speaking today, we have decided to give these young people an opportunity to bear their testimonies. And frankly, I'm afraid they will not do this, but that they will get up and leave this meetinghouse."

"President," I replied, "do not cut our young people so short. I promise you that will never happen. But I'm going to ask you, when you invite them to bear their testimonies, to have them come up to the front and bear their testimonies over the microphone."

The president smiled and said, "Now I know you are out in left field. They will never do that."

I said, "President, if I had the authority today, that would be the order of this meeting."

Well, he finally acquiesced. And when the moment came for the testimony part of the meeting, he invited them to come up to the stand to speak.

As soon as he sat down, nearly one-fourth of the persons in the congregation stood up.

The stake president leaned over to me and said, "See, I told you they'd get up and go home."

"Yes, President, but you're greatly mistaken. They are not going in the direction of the doors."

They came up to the front of that room, took every vacant seat available, and filled all the choir seats. They sat on the steps and they sat on the floor in front of the platform guests. And after one or two had borne their testimonies, they started to rush to the pulpit for fear they would not get a chance. The president said to me, "What shall we do now?"

"Well, President, it is your job now to referee this thing."

So he moved his chair over by the pulpit and announced that he would point to the one who should next bear his testimony.

After several had borne their testimonies, he pointed to a girl and she arose with her sister, and both came to the pulpit. The older of the girls said; "Most of you know us very well. You know the family to which we belong. We have a testimony we wish to bear today.

"For a long time in our home our father and mother were social drinkers. They both smoked, and neither of them had ever offered a prayer in the home. They were good to us in a lot of ways, but not in the ways we cherished most. So we went to our seminary teachers and they advised on a certain procedure, which we decided to try.

"One evening at supper time we asked Dad if he would bless the food. He refused, and Mother refused. He said, 'If you want these meals of ours blessed, we will be willing to let you two do it.' So for some time we blessed the food in our home.

"One evening we asked our parents if they would please join us in a family home evening. Again our father said,

'Well, if you two girls will do the entertaining, I guess we can spare the time.' So we began to hold family home evenings.

"Finally we went to the bishop and asked him to help us by sending us home teachers. He promised he would. A night or two later, arrangements were made, and home teachers visited our home. What they said is beside the point, but the seeds were planted in good earth. It wasn't long after this that Father and Mother both stopped smoking. They stopped drinking. They accepted our invitation to come with us to church."

At this point the girl started to cry. She had to sit down, so her younger sister told the rest of the story:

"Last night, in the Salt Lake Temple," she said, "the greatest thing in the world happened to our family. My sister and I stood by while our parents, kneeling over the altar of the holy priesthood of God, were sealed together as man and wife for time and for eternity. Then my sister and I, placing our hands in theirs, were sealed to them forever as their daughters. They kissed us after it was over, and the person officiating said, 'Go right ahead and love each other, brother. This is the first time in your life that you have ever had your arms around your eternal wife and the first time that you parents have ever held your eternal daughters in your arms.' "

At the conclusion of this beautiful testimony, many others rushed to the front for the golden opportunity of testifying of their love of home and church.

Better to Be "Chicken"

Sin has an ugly face.

In one of the high schools in Utah County at one time, when I was a school supervisor, I visited the seminary in the forenoon. During the lunch hour I went into the hallways of the high school just to study human beings and get the spirit of youth again from their standpoint.

That day I was just in time to receive the students' school paper, which was then being distributed. I noticed students all along the walls of the corridors reading the paper. In a sort of secluded spot were two boys. They were of considerable stature, and I was not sure whether they were preparing to have a fight or what. So I eased myself over as near to them as I dared.

One boy, whom we'll call Bill, was trying to get his friend John to join him in some plot or game; something that was wrong, but he was promising his friend they would have a lot of fun. "Come on, John, come and go with me," he insisted.

But John said: "Now, wait a minute. I recall only about two weeks ago in our home evening my father talked about this very thing you're asking me to do. It's evil, and he showed us how wrong it would be. So I'll just have to tell you, Bill, that under no conditions will I go with you. Not on your life. The Lord has given me two legs to stand on, two feet to move me about, and I tell you I'm going to use them for my own defense."

Bill persisted, saying, "Aw, come on, chicken."

Finally John became angry. "Listen, Bill. I'd like you to know one other thing. Not too long ago we had a discussion in our family home evening about being 'chicken.' And my dad said how wonderful it is, in the eyes of God, for someone who is out in a car or some place with the gang to have the courage and strength to stand up against the crowd and say no. And he said that those who won't do that are showing the height of stupidity to fall in line with wrong pressures. So let me tell you something — you go right ahead and do this thing. I'd rather be 'chicken' !"

What a great feeling I had then to go up to that boy and throw my arms around him and give him a squeeze! One who stands above the crowd, who isn't afraid to say no to temptations and to stand up for what he believes, is greatly magnified and blessed. May we all have the strength and stamina and courage to say no when we are tempted.

The Rewards of Repentance

To bolster up the standards in our home stake at one time, we as a stake presidency planned an intensive local missionary program. We knew the risks we were taking. We were looking for fishermen to be our representatives — men who had never fished. We located about fifteen such men who, with encouragement, might know more about the problems of our stake than anyone else, men who knew the people, the farms, the social structure. We issued formal calls to these brethren and each one responded.

The stake presidency had prepared an appropriate meeting for the occasion. We all bore our testimony, then set each man apart. One brother asked if he might be the last one to have this official honor. As the others in the group left the meeting-place, this brother broke down and cried. He stated that he had drunk coffee since he was fourteen years old. He had smoked since he was sixteen years old. He had attended church but little. His tithing record was nearly zero. Then he said; "Brethren, I am morally clean. I think much of my fellowmen, and I believe the Joseph Smith story. Now, would you like to take a chance on me?"

Why not? we wondered. In our minds we were praying for the inspiration of our Heavenly Father to direct us. Then there came into my mind the words of Elder Melvin J. Ballard of the Council of the Twelve, spoken at one of our stake conferences. He said, "If I were the bishop of this ward, I would have a sign outside that read 'Welcome!' And on the first three rows of the meeting-room I would have signs saying 'For Smokers Only.' "

We told this dear brother that it was not within our province to tell him that he would be allowed to do the things he had enumerated and still be a missionary, but we would pray for him and ask a willing Father for the help he needed. He gratefully accepted the challenge.

After two months of missionary work he called and asked for permission to visit our home. The meeting was arranged. With fear and trembling, he stood up and bore his testimony. Said he, "Since I was set apart, I have never tasted tea, coffee, or alcoholic beverages, nor have I used tobacco in any form." He sealed his speech with his tears. Then he made the following remark, which to me was more powerful than his testimony: "President Anderson, I want you all to know something else that is a miracle to me. I have never even been tempted to use these things any more."

How glorious is the promise of the Lord, who said, " . . . prove me now herewith . . . if I will not open you the windows of heaven, and pour you out a blessing, that there shall not be room enough to receive it." (Malachi 3:10.) This man's wife and son have secretly thanked us many times, for their family was brought much closer together because of the call of their husband and father.

True Parentage

My mother and father never had their pictures in the newspaper or a magazine, but they were two of the loveliest people who ever blessed this earth by their marvelous spirituality and their love for their family. In our home each of the children — there were eight of us — was prepared before baptism for the importance of that event in our lives. One of the most memorable experiences of my life was my own baptism.

My father took me by horse and buggy to the Manti Temple for the occasion. We had traveled about halfway there when the horse suddenly refused to go any further. He stopped and just wouldn't go on. My father got out with a whip and tuned the horse up a little. Finally he jumped back into the buggy again and we went on our way rejoicing, wondering what had happened and why.

After the baptism service we returned to our home in Ephraim, and my father set me on his lap and said, "Leland, I have news for you."

"Oh, Father, let's hear it," I exclaimed.

He said, "I want you to know that I am your father."

I smiled in answer to that. "I never doubted that for a minute," I said.

"And," he added, "I want you to know that your mother is your mother."

I said, "Thank the Lord for that."

Then he went on, "Today at the temple I want you to know what happened to you. You are now a full-fledged member of The Church of Jesus Christ of Latter-day Saints. Citizenship in the kingdom of God is now yours to have and to hold for time and eternity, if you will. Also, I want you to know that from the day you were born until this day, you were sort of lent to us by the Lord. Your name was entered on the Church records today, and it is there for keeps."

What a wonderful thing that has been in my life! My father assured me that my person belonged to him and my mother: we three were now one flesh forever. What an objective to work from and to! How wonderful to be worthy of blessings like that, true parentage!

Five years later my father passed away with pneumonia. I shall never forget his last words before he died. He called me into his bedroom and, with great difficulty, said to me, "Leland, I guess last night was my last night on this earth. Be good to your mother. And when I get into the spirit world I'll do my best to get permission to meet you when you die, to be the first one to meet you there."

What a marvelous thing it is to have a father and a mother who can enjoy companionship with all of their children, thus helping them to be identified in the family circle and know where they all belong. I only hope that my father will be permitted to meet me when I die, as he suggested, and that I will be worthy of that same blessing in relation to my own children.

Not the Least Degree of Allowance

Walking on top of middle mountain up Sterling Canyon is a beautiful experience. Deer play hide and seek on this timberland during deer-hunting season. But to be caught or trapped on this high plateau in a blizzard calls for the use of one's keenest senses as well as for outside help.

I was so engulfed one fall season. After a couple of hours of fruitless effort to locate help or a camp, I experienced some fear. I shot my gun five times in rapid succession — and heard an answer immediately and less than a hundred yards away.

The snow and hail were blinding, but I found a friendly camp where I was invited in. There, sitting on their bunks, were five cold deer hunters. All were thawing out by a stove in the center of the tent. The thawing out was greatly enhanced by a steaming cup of coffee in the hands of each of them.

The leader of the group was my cousin, so I asked him if I might have a cup with them. He responded with, "Leland, you are the stake president of everyone in this tent. You will enjoy a cup of coffee over my dead body."

A joking atmosphere prevailed, as each made excuses for himself. They only drank coffee while deer hunting, I was told. Then I talked to them about double standards in the Church, and that the gospel is a straight and narrow path with no degree of allowance for any of us. "If ye are not one, ye are not mine," the Lord said.

They agreed that there should be no double standards, and I settled for a cup of "Mormon tea" — a cup of hot milk with sugar in it.

The day ended well, with success in finding deer. It also ended well in other respects, for there was repentance on the part of some of those men. I am truly thankful for and do truly believe in section 89 of the Doctrine and Covenants, the Lord's great law of health.

A House Left Desolate

One evening in the mountains of the Wasatch Range in Utah, a number of friends were enjoying an evening together in a remote cabin. Each couple had prepared a splendid dish for the menu, and we were all lighthearted as we discussed many subjects. Near the close of the party, our discussion ventured into the area of the spiritual, and many expressed thankful hearts for the revealed truths we live by.

At this moment one couple asked for quiet as they revealed to us their newly adopted faith. As we listened, we were shocked and speechless. It was like the children of Israel disowning God and Samuel. Their future course, they said, was to be a quiet duet. No more church for them. No more tithes or offerings. No more meetings. They would treat all people as they hoped to be treated, live a good life, and harm no one. What a marvelous future they envisioned — just basking in the sunshine with no responsibility! Then they asked their shocked audience to respond to their version of their new faith.

When it came my turn to respond, I answered, "If Lucifer has a set of articles of faith, that must be his first one. If each person on the earth should follow suit, it would in a moment destroy the Church, God, and the meaning of life."

So pressing was this problem in Christ's own time that he made it the subject of a long speech to his followers, which is recorded in the twenty-third chapter of Matthew. He warned his followers against heedless discipleship. To drive out false masters from the soul and leave one's house a personality unoccupied by higher effort would be disaster. He taught that moral neutrality is everywhere in imminent peril. Negative virtue is not a city of peace — it is beleaguered on every hand. The tragedy of this type of philosophy is its emptiness. Then he concluded, "Behold, your house is left unto you desolate. For I say unto you, Ye shall not see me henceforth, till ye shall say, Blessed is he that cometh in the name of the Lord." (Matthew 23:38-39.)

Henry Wadsworth Longfellow's poem "Holy Spirit, Truth Divine" gives us a new type of hope here, for in some of his lines we find the following:

> *Holy spirit, right divine,*
> *King within my conscience reign.*
> *Be my law and I shall be*
> *Firmly bound, forever free.*

Don't Hang Around the Gate

Dr. George Brimhall, former president of Brigham Young University, once told an impressive story that has been a guide to me ever since I heard it.

He was on an assignment to Canada, and while there was invited to go out to see one of the beautiful herds of cattle on the range. The cattle were feeding on well-fenced acreage. With a keen eye, President Brimhall noticed three distinct groups of cattle. One group was running up and down the fence line; another group was meandering around the gate; and the third group, comprising about 90 percent of the herd, was out in the pasture, knee deep in grass.

President Brimhall's host was asked to explain this phenomenon. "Well," he said, "as you see, we call group one fence-runners, group two gate-hangers, and group three feeders. We lose money on those that are poor in flesh in the first two groups, but as you will notice, the feeders are fat and ready for market."

President Brimhall, being of poetic temperament, wrote these challenging lines, titled "Long and Short Range Arrows":

> *Oh, my soul, be up and doing,*
> *Up and feeding,*
> *Feeding early,*
> *Feeding late;*
> *Never running along the fences,*
> *Never hanging around the gate.*

The Lesson of Love

A few years ago I was privileged to have in my New Testament class at Brigham Young University my own daughter and her best friend. They were students at the Brigham Young High School on the lower campus and took a religion class at the university.

Teaching was just part of my assignment at that time, for I was also chairman of the two assembly programs held each week at the university.

One special week our assembly speaker was to be President David O. McKay, whose subject was the second great commandment. On the morning of that assembly, these two girls came into my office, asking for a special privilege. Though the high school students were not allowed to attend the assemblies, they wanted special permission to do so because they had three important questions they wished to ask President McKay.

We debated the issue for a few moments and finally I gave permission on these conditions: they were to sit on the front row, and as soon as the assembly was over, they were to rush up to President McKay and ask him the questions.

In talking with my wife later that morning I mentioned this experience, and we speculated on whether or not the girls would ask the questions. Finally I said, "Mother, I will wager you that they will never ask one question. If they do, I will buy you a new dress; and if they don't, you will buy me a new suit." She agreed.

I had a reserved seat at the assembly, beside President McKay. What a glorious spiritual feast we had! Then, as soon as the meeting was concluded, the girls put in their appearance beside the prophet. They looked up into his piercing eyes, and he put his arms about them. Then they broke down in tears, and tears from the prophet also trickled down his cheeks. They stood that way for a few seconds, and then the spell was broken. "Bless you, bless you," he said. The girls then left the scene, highly elated at the victory won.

The prophet had taught well the lesson of love, the lesson his life portrayed. In his presence the girls felt it deeply. Further words were unnecessary.

"Rescue That Boy"

One evening when I was serving as stake president in Manti, Utah, Brother Roscoe Eardley of Salt Lake City, a member of the Church Welfare Committee, stayed at our home. He related the following memorable story to us:

He was returning home from a welfare meeting late one evening, going east on Fourth South Street in Salt Lake City. As he approached Main Street, he noticed a soldier and a young woman walking along the street, with the young woman seeming to pull her companion along with her. Brother Eardley smiled to himself as he passed them. But when he had gone about half a block further, he seemed to hear a voice say to him, "Brother Eardley, turn your car around and go back and rescue that young man from that woman."

He did not hesitate; he about-faced and soon was pulling up to the side of the street where the woman was still pulling the soldier along with her.

Brother Eardley jumped out of his car, went up to them both, and said, "'Young lady, I am sorry, but this man is my prisoner. You will just have to give him to me." She objected strenuously, but soon Brother Eardley had the soldier in his car with him and the woman went on down the street crying.

As they drove along, the soldier explained that he was stationed at Fort Douglas, a military reservation east of Salt Lake City. When asked how he happened to be in the company of a woman of questionable morals, he explained: "To-night, for some reason, I felt very lonely up at the Fort, and

I thought I would go downtown to see if I could find something to cheer me up. I had heard that the Mormons were wonderful people and that this was a good town. As I was walking down Main Street, I heard jazzy music being played below in a basement room. I just went down the stairway and found a dancing party going on. I stood and watched for a few minutes, when a couple came up to me and asked me to join them. So I did."

He recalled that it wasn't long until he wished he had stayed at the Fort. Liquor was flowing freely at the party and he soon found himself inebriated. Then the young woman approached him and suggested they get some fresh air. He soon found her urging him on, but he was too drunk to realize what was happening. That was when Brother Eardley came by and rescued him.

Brother Eardley took him to his home, helped revive his spirits as best he could, and asked him to spend the night there. The soldier declined, however, as he noticed with alarm that he was due back at Fort Douglas in an hour. Brother Eardley drove him back to the Fort. He also assured the young man that the Mormon people *were* some of the best people on earth, and that Salt Lake City was a fine place in which to live. He insisted that the soldier came to spend the next weekend with the Eardley family.

When he arrived at Brother Eardley's home that weekend, the soldier had dinner with the family, who then showed him around the city. He was invited to spend each weekend with this gracious family.

About two weeks later the soldier arrived, almost out of breath. He had news from his family in Pennsylvania. "Mr. Eardley," he said, "I want you to read a letter from my mother."

In the letter, the mother told her son about a terrible dream she had had a few nights before. She named the night, and it was the very night Brother Eardley had met the young man downtown. She said she woke up suddenly and saw in a sort of vision that her son was in great danger. She got down on her knees and pleaded with the Lord to save her son. In noting the time this took place, Brother Eardley discovered that the woman was praying for her son at the exact time a voice told him, "Go back and rescue that boy."

What a wonderful letter! Jesus said, "For he that is not against us is on our part." (Mark 9:40.) He told Peter and his other followers not to stop people from doing good, for it would all redound to the good of the Church. (Mark 9: 38-41.) We are all of one parenthood — children of the Father. He answers the sincere, earnest prayer. May we each live lives of such merit that we can entertain revelations, as Brother Eardley did, and walk within the light of that which is revealed to us.

The Hidden Curriculum

I had a wonderful experience in the seminary at Spanish Fork, Utah. I had just listened to one of our fine student trainees give his last class at the end of his six-week training period. He then sealed his testimony with the story of his birth, which his parents had many times related to him. His mother had nearly given her life for him to come to this earth, but answers to prayer and the power of the holy priesthood had saved her life as well as the baby's.

He concluded five minutes before the bell was to ring, and, not knowing what to do with the extra time, he thanked the students and told them they might sit and quietly whisper to each other until the bell rang. At this moment one of the boys raised his hand.

What would you say is the choicest curriculum in the class? It is not the printed page. It is the choice moments like the ones that followed.

The boy asked the teacher if he might stand up and speak. The permission was granted, and the boy stood with quivering chin for a moment before he could speak. Then he told his story:

"You all know me. For a long time I was the only child in our family. But a few months ago my parents told me, 'Son, we have some good news. We are going to have a baby.'

"I was so thrilled, I practically shouted. Then I lay at night in bed planning. If it was a sister, I would defend her always, take her to dances, champion her in society. If it were a brother, I'd plan fishing and hunting trips with him, and help him be worthy of holding the priesthood and serving on a mission.

"Well, the event finally came. We all three went to the hospital, and I waited with my father. Things didn't go well, though, and for three or four days the doctors were not sure they would be able to save either the baby or my mother.

"One night my father and I went home, after hearing that things were still critical in the hospital, and we wept on each other's shoulder. Then I said, 'Dad, do we have to stand by and take this on the chin?'

" 'Well, what do you suggest doing?' he asked.

" 'Haven't we got any consecrated oil in the house?'

" 'Yes,' my father said, and we grabbed it and rushed back to the hospital."

The boy paused to wipe tears away from his eyes, then continued: "In the hospital we administered first to my mother and asked God to spare her life. Then we administered to my little brother and asked the Lord to please spare his life also.

"Oh, brothers and sisters, I invite you to come over to our home and see us. All of us are well and strong. All of us are here. The Prince of Peace granted to our home a stay of death and a new lease on life and happiness. And I ask God to help me keep the promises that I made in my daydreams to my brother by seeing him on his way happily devoted to the work of the Lord."

Love Unfeigned

Oftentimes we need to be reminded of the importance of love. It is like a well; it can run dry. It is like a fire; it is all-consuming. It is like a seed; it needs to be nourished and fed. And it is like a rose in the fall; it can be killed by a frost.

I remember an experience in my own family that helped chart the direction I was to take in my later life. My father and two of his brothers, my Uncle Lewis and Uncle Will, owned a sizeable field. It had one fence around it. I was never quite sure which acres belonged to my father and which ones to my uncles. They used the same horses, the same machinery, and most often helped each other in the harvests. This was family togetherness if ever there was such a thing. We existed by virtue of each other.

Years later, while attending the Brigham Young University, I remember hearing a poem read by a beloved teacher, Dr. George Brimhall, that brought the hills of home to my soul. Dr. Brimhall felt the title of the poem should be "Love Unfeigned," but the author called it "Abram and Zimri."

Abram and Zimri owned a field together,
A level field in a Happy Vale.
They plowed it with one plow,
And in the spring sowed, walking side by side,
The fruitful seed.

In harvest when the glad earth
Smiled with grain,

Each carried to his home
One-half the sheaves,
And stored them with much labor in his barns.

Now Abram had a wife and seven sons,
But Zimri dwelt alone within his house.
One night before the sheaves were gathered in,
As Zimri lay upon his lonely bed
And counted in his mind his little gains,
He thought upon his brother Abram's lot and said,
"I dwell alone within my house, but
Abram hath a wife and seven sons;
And yet we share the harvest sheaves alike.
He surely needeth more for life than I;
I will arise and gird myself, and go down to the field
And add to his from mine."

So he arose and girded up his loins,
And went out softly to the level field.
The moon shone out from dusky bars of clouds,
And trees stood black against the cold blue sky;
The branches waved and whispered in the wind.
So Zimri, guided by the shifting light,
Went down the mountain path and found the field,
Took from his store of sheaves a generous third,
And bore them gladly to his brother's heap,
And then went back to sleep and happy dreams.

Now the same night, as Abram lay in bed,
Thinking upon his blissful state of life,
He thought upon his brother Zimri's lot and said,
"He dwells within his house alone;
He goeth forth to toil with few to help.
He goeth home at night to a cold house,
And hath few other friends but me and mine,
But these two till the Happy Vale alone,
While I whom heaven hath very greatly blessed
Dwell happy with my wife and seven sons,
Who aid me in my toil and make it light,
And yet we share the harvest sheaves alike.
This surely is not pleasing unto God.

I will arise and gird myself, and go out to the field,
And borrow from my store, and add unto my brother
      Zimri's pile."

So he arose and girded up his loins
And went softly down to the level field.
The moon shone out from silver bars of clouds,
The trees stood black against the starry sky,
The dark leaves waved and whispered in the breeze.
So Abram, guided by the doubtful light,
Passed down the mountain path and found the field,
Took from his sheaves a generous third,
And added them unto his brother's heap.
Then he went back to sleep and happy dreams.

The next morning with the early sun
The brothers arose and went out to their toil.
And when they came to see the heavy sheaves,
Each wondered in his heart to find his heap,
Though he had given a third, was still the same.

Now the next night went Zimri to the field,
Took from his store of sheaves a generous third,
And placed them on his brother Abram's heap,
Then lay down behind the pile to watch.
The moon looked out from bars of silvery clouds,
The cedars stood out black against the sky,
The olive branches whispered softly in the wind.
Then Abram came down softly from his home,
And looking to the left and right went on,
Took from his ample store a generous third,
And lay it on his brother Zimri's pile.

Then Zimri arose, and caught him in his arms,
And wept upon his cheek, and kissed his cheek,
And Abram saw the whole and could not speak.
Neither could Zimri, for their hearts were full.

The Address of Jesus

"And there was a certain disciple at Damascus, named Ananias; and to him said the Lord in a vision, Ananias. And he said, Behold, I am here, Lord.

"And the Lord said unto him, Arise, and go into the street which is called Straight, and inquire in the house of Judas for one called Saul, of Tarsus: for, behold, he prayeth,

"And hath seen in a vision a man named Ananias coming in, and putting his hand on him, that he might receive his sight." (Acts 9:10-12.)

Paul never forgot this address. He never forgot that here he found his Lord and Savior.

When John and Andrew asked the Lord, "Where do you live?" he replied, "Come and see." To the Samaritan woman at the well of Jacob, Jesus said that neither Jerusalem nor Samaria was the place to worship, but that true worshippers would worship the Father in spirit and in truth.

A few years ago I read in a magazine the story of a Christmas program in the Midwest. The city council asked one of the town's first citizens to be in charge of Christmas cheer in this fine Christian community. Every home must be visited; everyone would be invited to contribute.

The chairman prayed for divine inspiration, and each home was visited. He informed everyone that on Monday next he would be at home, sitting near his telephone, from eight in the morning until five in the afternoon. He invited everyone in town who could do so to call and tell him if they knew the address of Jesus Christ.

At 8:30 in the morning the first call came. An elderly widow said she knew the address he was seeking. He said, "Please hold on while I get a pencil and some paper. Okay, what is it?"

"Brother John," she said, "the Savior's address is in my heart and it is also in my home." This was the story of the widow's mite all over again. Then she said, "What may I give the community? I have no money, but I have extra clothing, extra bedding, bottles of fruit, and canned meat. Please let me help."

In Christ's time, Jesus pointed out the widow's mite as the greatest gift. What would he have said of this generous widow?

Two weeks after I read this story, it was Christmastime in Provo, Utah. William A. Tolman, a seminary teacher of great faith, told me of the desire of his students to do a real Christmas service. I told him about the story I had read, and this set us both in motion.

In our ward lived a couple who had fled religious persecution in one of the iron curtain countries. Through trials and heartaches they were able to travel to America, their new home of freedom. This couple, well along in years, were facing the Christmas season alone. But they would not be alone. The spirit of Christ compensated for the lack of family ties.

On Christmas Eve there was a knock at their door. As they opened the door, many voices rang out, "Merry Christmas, merry Christmas," followed by the singing of beautiful Christmas carols by the seminary students.

The youths were invited in, and into the room they brought a Christmas tree complete with lights, tinsel, decorations, candy, and presents galore. In moments it was set up. The lovely old couple embraced each other with tears streaming down their cheeks.

After more Christmas songs, the students quietly filed out, leaving the couple alone. Brother Tolman was the last one to leave, and the old couple asked, "Aren't you taking the tree and all of these presents with you?"

"Oh, no," he replied. "This all belongs to you. This is our Christmas gift to you."

The man and woman could no longer speak, for their hearts were full.

Who Is the Captain?

President William E. Berrett, director of seminaries and institutes, called me into his office one morning and asked if I would accept an assignment, the like of which I had never before had in my life. I answered, "Yes, providing you feel that I have sufficient stature for the occasion."

He then told me that the University of Arizona at Flagstaff annually holds what they call a "Week of Religious Enlightenment." Leaders of many different religions are invited to participate. Each day the speakers go to assigned rooms and students come to question them about their faith. President Berrett said to me, "Now, Leland, all you have to do is to go to the class concerned, stand before them, announce yourself a Mormon, then say, 'What would you like to know about The Church of Jesus Christ of Latter-day Saints?' "

Each evening for seven days I was also to speak primarily to local institute of religion students; however, all the students from the university were invited to be present. Frightened, I was on my knees every spare moment I had, preparing for this experience.

One day that week I faced a large science class. The teacher, a graduate of Brigham Young University, had fortified me a day in advance as to what to expect. I had in my possession three or four excellent speeches from Dr. Armand Hill, a scientist of great note from BYU. In fact, I almost memorized them.

The teacher had told his students that he would not tolerate any unprofessionalism on their part. He had also forewarned me that two students, both agnostics in the deepest sense of the word, would be on the front row and might cause a problem.

As I proceeded, the Holy Ghost and my prior preparation with the speeches of Dr. Hill upheld me and inspired me in this trial by faith. The two problem students showed little else than disagreement.

I closed my discussion by reading two poems. One was written by a journalist, William Ernest Henley, titled "Invictus." The other was written in response by an apostle of the Lord Jesus Christ, Elder Orson F. Whitney, titled "The Soul's Captain."

INVICTUS

Out of the night that covers me,
  Black as the Pit from pole to pole,
I thank whatever gods may be
  For my unconquerable soul.

In the fell clutch of circumstance
  I have not winced nor cried aloud.
Under the bludgeonings of chance
  My head is bloody, but unbowed.

Beyond this place of wrath and tears
  Looms but the horror of the shade,
And yet the menace of the years
  Finds, and shall find me, unafraid.

It matters not how strait the gate,
  How charged with punishments the scroll,
I am the master of my fate;
  I am the captain of my soul.

And the response:

THE SOUL'S CAPTAIN

Art thou in truth?
Then what of Him who bought thee with His blood?

Who plunged into devouring seas
And snatched thee from the flood?

Who bore for all our fallen race
What none but Him could bear,
The God who died that man might live
And endless glory share?

Of what avail thy vaunted strength
Apart from His vast might?
Pray that His light may pierce the gloom,
That thou may see aright.

Men are as bubbles on the waves,
As leaves upon the tree.
Thou captain of thy soul?
Forsooth, who gave that place to thee?

Free will is thine, free agency
To wield for right or wrong,
But thou must answer unto Him
To whom all souls belong.

Then bend to the dust that head unbowed,
Small part of life's great whole,
And see in Him, and Him alone,
The captain of thy soul.

At the close of the class, one of the agnostic students on the front row came rushing up and asked, "Where can I find those poems? How much would I have to pay for them? I am deeply concerned."

I looked directly at him. We clasped hands, and I said, "Brother, I am honored by your request. I here present them to you, free of charge." With a slight choke in his voice he thanked me very much.

Faith is like love. It cannot be forced. The Holy Ghost is like a calm morning: He brings peace and contentment to the soul.

A Brother and Sister's Love

In families where there are several children, I have noticed that the children sometimes seem to pair off, with two or three of them getting along better with each other than others in the family. I had a special feeling for one of my sisters. Her name was Ila.

Our friendship and closeness were real in our lives. Once when I went to teach school in Brigham City, Utah, my beloved sister, then about twelve years of age, contracted diphtheria. This led to heart trouble, and soon her life was hanging on a thread. Finally the doctor said to my mother, "If you want Leland to see her while she's still alive, you'd better send for him immediately."

That morning, as I had just rung the bell for my students to march into the building, the train depot agent rushed in and handed me a telegram. All it said was, "Hurry home, Ila is dying."

I immediately got someone to take my classes for the day, and I started out on foot for Ephraim, some two hundred miles south. In that day there were few automobiles, and I could not afford to wait for a train. So I started out on foot, catching rides as best I could, and arrived in Ephraim shortly after midnight. As I walked into the darkened house, my lovely sister Ila, who was sleeping in the parlor just off the front hall, heard my steps and cried out, "Leland!"

What a divine affinity! She even knew my footstep. I rushed into the room, turned on the light, and held her in my arms. Mother had heard the noise and came running in.

The very first thing Ila asked me was, "Leland, can you bless me alone without the help of some other man?"

"You bet I can, Ila," I said. I anointed her with consecrated oil and then blessed her with all my heart. I asked God — I pleaded with him — to let my sister live. While I was sealing the anointing, she fell asleep. After a while, as we watched her, she woke up and seemed to have a new lease on life. She smiled and cried at the same time.

"While you were blessing me," she said, "our father [who had been dead for a few years] appeared to me in a vision and said, 'Ila, I need you very much to help me here in the spirit world, to help with the records that we're working on of our family line. I have come for you, Ila. You are not to remain on earth much longer.' "

I stayed right by her side, holding her hand, and it was only a few minutes later that Ila looked up with a smile on her face and then passed to her reward.

How I long and hope that one day, when I am called home to meet my Maker, I will be privileged once more literally to embrace my beloved sister Ila.

Gospel Givers

I am indebted to President A. Theodore Tuttle of the First Council of the Seventy for the following story.

While he was teaching seminary in Brigham City, Utah, he said, he knew a wonderful bishop who owned many acres of land in the western part of the county. One year he was blessed with an exceptionally large crop. He had sold thousands of bushels of hard wheat. When he went out to get the last load from the threshing, with his big truck carrying about ten tons, he wondered what he would do with it. He had a big bank account, all his silos were filled with wheat, and thousands of bushels had been sold. He thought a while, then said, "I know what I'll do — I'll give it to Brother John."

Brother John, who lived in this bishop's ward, had just been married. He and his wife had built a large chicken coop and were raising white leghorn chickens so they would have eggs to sell.

The bishop felt that nothing would be better than to give this young couple a boost in life. I'm not unmindful of the rich man in the New Testament who had a similar experience, except that his experience ended terribly. When he looked at his crops and all his barns loaded, he said to himself, "What will I do with all this increase? I know what I will do; I will tear my barns down and will build bigger ones. I will load them with the fruits of my labors." This man had forgotten to distinguish between what was the Lord's and what was his.

So the bishop drove up to the home of Brother John, backed his truck into the lot, and went up and knocked on the door. When he found there was no one home, he said, "Thank the Lord." Then he backed up against the big empty silo and put the machinery to work, and it wasn't long until he had the silo nearly filled with wheat. Then he drove off.

Two or three weeks passed. One day he met the young man on the sidewalk downtown. Brother John said to him, "Bishop, I have a problem. Someone by mistake has emptied a load of wheat and filled my silo. Now my chickens got into some of it this morning, and they sure like it, but I'm sure some farmer had a helper who didn't know where to unload it and put it in my granary by mistake. I'm wondering, inasmuch as you're a farmer, if you know anyone else who's been hauling grain into town."

With a twinkle in his eye, the bishop responded: "Brother John, if I were you, I would never try to find out who that man was."

Then Brother John realized the answer. He grabbed the bishop by the hand and said, "God bless you, dear bishop. I think I knew all the time who had done that work." The young man whipped out his checkbook, opened it, got out a pen, and started to write out a check. "How much do I owe you for that wheat?" he asked.

The bishop said, "John, put that checkbook back in your pocket. And as long as you live, don't think you owe me anything. If you live to be a million years old, you could not pay me for that wheat."

So both of them went on their way, rejoicing in the commandment of the Lord to love your neighbor as yourself.

A couple of weeks later was Thanksgiving, and the bishop went down to the meat locker to get some choice meat for Thanksgiving dinner. As he opened the door, he saw that the locker was filled with dressed chickens. He smiled, took what he needed, and went on his way with a lighter step.

A week later he met John on the street and said, "John, I have a problem. Someone by mistake has put a lot of dressed chickens in one of my meat lockers. And since you're in the chicken business, I thought you might know who's been killing chickens around town, because I want to pay for them."

John replied, "Bishop, if I were you I would never try to find out." At that, the bishop pulled out of his pocketbook a roll of bills and started to peel off some of the big ones. But John said, "You put that money back in your pocket. If you live to be a million years old, you couldn't pay me for those chickens."

This is the true spirit of the gospel of Jesus Christ.

Commissioned of Jesus Christ

In Dallas, Texas, many years ago, while I was serving a mission there, I had an experience that has long remained in my memory.

After a street meeting one evening, as we were returning to our home, we passed a block that was lined with automobiles and at the end of which was a large tent packed with hundreds of people. We made our way to the tent, and just as we entered we noticed up at the front a canvas baptismal font partially filled with water. A minister of the Church of Christ was leading a young girl down into the water for baptism. As he stood in the water by her side, he said, "Having been commissioned of Jesus Christ, I baptize you in the name of the Father, and of the Son, and of the Holy Ghost. Amen."

My companions and I looked at each other in amazement. I said, "I didn't know there was another LDS Church in this town."

After the meeting we went up and introduced ourselves to the persons in charge. And that is how I met Dr. Eugene V. Wood, a dentist in Dallas. We had a long conversation about the gospel, and we found that their beliefs resembled our own in many respects. However, we also found some differences. So Dr. Wood invited me to come and see him in his office. One day I did, using as an excuse the fact that I needed to have a tooth fixed. Again we went into the beliefs we both espoused.

Later I went to his office for more extensive work on my teeth. This time he put a sort of bridle on my face which held my mouth open, so I couldn't respond to his comments. All the while he was grinding and filling, he kept shooting questions at me.

"Now I'll tell you one thing about the Book of Mormon," he said. "I don't believe a word of it." (Later he confessed to me that he had never read it.) "I can't believe it," he continued. "Now I know that at the present time we have no explanation for that book. But the day will come, I promise you, when we'll have the answer for it. When we do receive that answer from God, it won't be a very promising one for you."

Then he continued with his questions: "Mr. Anderson, what are you Mormon people going to do with all the people who have lived and died without the law? Are you going to send them to hell where they'll be burned forever, like many of the Protestant churches claim? What are you going to do about the honest in heart in our own day and time who have never even heard the name Jesus Christ? Are you going to send them to hell? You know, Mr. Anderson, we're not as dumb in the gospel as you people are, for we believe implicitly that the day will come somehow when the Lord will make it possible for them to hear the gospel of Jesus Christ and to be glorified for it."

And he went on and on, asking me questions, which he'd answer himself, always smiling, and all I could do was grunt and make motions.

Finally he took that bridle from my face, and I stood up and said; "Dr. Wood, you get in that chair. I'm going to be the interrogator now for a few moments. You asked me what we're going to do with all the people who have lived and died without the law. Let me assure you that a Mormon is the only person you could ask that question of and find the correct answer. What do you suspect that we do in our Mormon temples?"

I explained to him the saving ordinances of God that would help us redeem the dead, how we're baptized for the dead, how we have families sealed to each other, and the whole program of vicarious work for the dead. He was quite astonished to think that we had such a program.

Then I said to him (as I have on many other occasions to other persons with whom I discuss the gospel), "Brother Wood, what do they do in your temples?"

Taken aback, he said, "Well, I don't know that we do anything. I didn't know that we had any temples."

"You haven't," I said. "What did you do with them? They were on the earth in the time of Christ. They were built in Old Testament days. And they are being built in this dispensation of time." And I bore to him my testimony.

A few days later I received a letter from him. He said that he was highly pleased with what he had heard and he invited me to be a guest and sit on the platform at a big meeting to be held for the Church of Christ. He wanted me to be there to hear a Mr. Armstrong speak on authority and the priesthood of God. This I promised to do. The evening of the meeting I was there and listened very attentively to Mr. Armstrong's fine sermon on authority and the priesthood of God.

Among other things, he told this story: One day someone knocked at his door, and when he answered it, there stood a soldier in a U.S. Army uniform. He was selling a magazine called the *Literary Digest*. He said he was working his way through college, and he was taking subscriptions to this magazine, which was $4.00 a year.

Mr. Armstrong said, "All right, my boy, I'll subscribe to your magazine." He gave the young man the $4.00 and received a receipt in return. After several months, when the magazine had not yet arrived, he wrote to the main office of the magazine and complained about it. He received a reply that the magazine had no salesmen in the field taking subscriptions and that the person who had taken the money had done so without authority. Furthermore, they could not afford to reimburse him for the lost $4.00, for they had received numerous complaints of the same kind.

This became a sort of pivot for Mr. Armstrong to which he referred during the rest of his address. "Now, let's analyze this for a moment," he said. "The home office of the magazine was okay; the magazine was a recognized publication of importance; but here is an unauthorized servant. And naturally the home office cannot accept the responsibility for making good for what this impostor in the field does.

"You know," he continued, "the kingdom of God is like that. The home office, God, is all right. We all believe in him. The gospel of Jesus Christ and the plan of salvation, his magazine, are certainly all right. But we simply cannot accept the deeds done by many people on earth who act in the name of religion if they have not been authorized to perform the duties that they perform from day to day."

At the end of the meeting, Dr. Wood introduced me to Mr. Armstrong as his Mormon friend. Mr. Armstrong looked at me a moment as he held my hand, then said, "Well, Mr. Anderson, what did you think of my talk?"

I said, "It was certainly one of the most persuasive talks I have heard on authority. I was very impressed. And I wonder if you would give me permission, in my future talks on authority, to use the same example that you did."

"By all means," he said. "Go right ahead and use it. I think it is a good one. Now tell me honestly, straight from your heart, what you thought of my talk."

I surmised that he knew more about Mormonism than I had at first guessed. "I'd like to ask you a personal question first," I said. "And I don't want you to be offended. I won't ask it unless you promise me you won't be offended."

"I promise I will not be offended," he said.

Then I looked him straight in the eye and said, "Mr. Armstrong, aren't you that magazine agent?"

He immediately turned red and demanded, "What do you mean?"

I said, "Tell me, who authorized you to preach this sermon tonight? Paul tells us in Hebrews that 'no man taketh this honor unto himself, but he that is called of God, as was Aaron.' Were you called of God as was Aaron, by revelation, to perform the work?"

"No," he said, "not by revelation. But I do have authority to do this work."

"From where does it stem?" I asked.

He took out his Bible and turned to 2 Timothy, chapter 4, and read the first three verses:

"I charge thee therefore before God, and the Lord Jesus Christ, who shall judge the quick and the dead at his appearing and his kingdom;

"Preach the word; be instant in season, out of season; reprove, rebuke, exhort with all longsuffering and doctrine.

"For the time will come when they will not endure sound doctrine; but after their own lusts shall they heap to themselves teachers, having itching ears."

"By that scripture and through the Spirit of God," said Mr. Armstrong, "I am called to preach the gospel of Jesus Christ. There is my authority."

I said to him: "I am told that there are three billion people in the world. If half of them are men (even assuming you discount the ladies), then that's one and a half billion who could do the very same thing that you've done. They can open the Bible to Timothy and read that same message of Paul to go ahead and preach to save the souls of men. And by the same token they could take upon themselves the authority to go and preach. Then overnight, theoretically at least, we'd have one and a half billion churches in the world."

This was more than he could take. Finally he looked at me and said, "Then where did you get your authority?"

I said, "Mr. Armstrong, I have been standing here praying with all my heart that you would ask me that question. Now listen carefully. Jesus Christ received his authority from God by divine investiture of authority. Peter, James, and John, in their days on earth, received this authority from the Lord and Savior, Jesus Christ.

"In 1829 Joseph Smith and Oliver Cowdery received from Peter, James, and John the holy Melchizedek Priesthood and the apostleship. Other men were ordained, such as Martin Harris, and David Whitmer to hold this holy priesthood, and they ordained Brigham Young an apostle in 1835. He ordained George Q. Cannon an apostle in 1860. Heber J. Grant received the apostleship in 1882 from George Q. Cannon. And Leland E. Anderson, yours truly, received his present priesthood office in 1935 from President Heber J. Grant.

"These are my answers to you, Mr. Armstrong. The authority of the holy priesthood I hold has come down through the Lord Jesus Christ through his prophets, seers, and revelators right through this present age to me. And through that authority I officiate in his Church. Now what have you to say about this?"

Mr. Armstrong turned on his heel and left me standing with Dr. Wood. I turned to the dentist and said, "Now, brother, as soon as you get ready for baptism, you let me know. And I'll promise you that for once in your life you will be baptized by one who holds the authority of the priesthood to perform that ordinance in this the dispensation of the fulness of times."

Reconciliation

President Oscar A. Kirkham of the First Council of the Seventy once related in a conference an experience that made an impression on me.

He told of a dear friend in Salt Lake City who called him on the telephone one evening and said: "Brother Kirkham, I have lost my only son. He refuses to be directed by me any longer. He will not recognize me as his father. Whenever I speak to him, he gets up and walks out of the house. Please, Brother Kirkham, can you help me?"

Brother Kirkham said he would be delighted to help in any way he could. The man said that there was only one really good thing that his boy was still doing: he was still attending Sunday School, even though he didn't take much part in it. "If you would please find it convenient to go to Sunday School in our ward this Sunday," the man said, "perhaps you can catch up with my boy as he starts home and walk along with him and talk with him."

Brother Kirkham promised he would. That Sunday, he found it convenient to sit in the same class as the boy. He found it convenient to leave the building at the same time as the boy and to walk home with him. As they walked along, Brother Kirkham asked, "My boy, how is everything in your home?"

"Oh, fine, I guess."

"Now wait a minute. Look right at me and tell me, is everything fine?"

Finally the boy broke down and said, "Brother Kirkham, we're having a terrible time in our home. My father and I, it seems, have very little in common. And I was wondering if you would be willing to do me a great favor."

Brother Kirkham answered, "Indeed I will."

"Could I get you to please speak to my father?"

What an invitation! How it all had been manipulated so beautifully! Inspired? Yes.

Brother Kirkham put his arm around the boy and said, "You bet I'll talk to your father, and to you too."

As they reached the home, they went into a private room — the father, his son, and Brother Kirkham — and spent a most profitable hour together. It was the return of the prodigal, in a sense, for both father and son were guilty.

Brother Kirkham said, "What we really did in that room was no one's business. But when we came out, all three of us were in tears. The father and the son had their arms around each other, and peace has reigned ever since in that lovely family."

Oh, what saviors we can be to our loved ones if we will!

No Offering Too Great

President Heber J. Grant once told a story that made a great impression on his listeners. It was later reprinted in the *Improvement Era*. This is the story:

A convert to the Church in Denmark had emigrated to Utah but was not paying his tithes and offerings. One evening a couple of boys called at his home and said that they had been sent by the bishop to collect fast offerings.

"What on earth do you mean by fast offerings?" he asked. "I never heard of it."

They explained that once a month all Saints go without a couple of meals for a day and contribute for the poor the money that they would have spent on food.

Well, the man grumbled for a bit and finally gave them a small offering.

Later the bishop called upon the man and said, "Now you've lived among us for three or four months, and I notice that you've never paid any tithing."

"Tithing! Good heavens, what's that?"

"Why, don't you know what tithing is? Didn't those who converted you tell you about it?"

"No, they never mentioned any tithing to me."

So the bishop referred the convert to Malachi 3, wherein the Lord commands his people to pay tithing.

"Well," the man said, "how much do I owe this time?"

The bishop informed him that a proper tithe would be one-tenth of his monthly earnings, and that from such funds the Church is operated.

Well, the Danish convert was very disappointed. He felt that he and not the Lord was being robbed. But after the bishop explained to him what the money was used for, he finally agreed and said, "Bishop, I'll try to be a good tithe payer."

Later he received from a committee in the ward a letter about an assessment for ward maintenance. Again he balked, but he finally consented to pay it.

About this time his son decided to go to Brigham Young University, where he became an excellent student. The reports that were received by his parents were most pleasing. One day the bishop again called on the Danish convert and said to him, "We've been watching your son, and we think he would make a wonderful missionary. We would recommend your son for a two-year mission."

Startled, the man said, "Who will pay for it?"

The bishop replied, "Why, we will give *you* the right to pay all of his expenses and keep him there during the two years that he is on a mission. The only thing the Church can afford to pay will be his ticket back home to Zion."

This was the straw that broke the camel's back. At first the father flatly refused. He had given all he could give, and he couldn't afford one cent more.

The bishop, a wise man who knew his ward members well, said, "Well, now, brother, let's forget it. Let's talk about something else." So they had a nice visit together. Then in the course of the conversation he asked, "How did you happen to join the Church?"

The convert replied, "One night in Copenhagen my wife and I heard a knock at our door, and there stood two Mormon missionaries. Oh, bishop, you'll never know how grateful we are to the Lord for those two wonderful boys, for they brought salvation to us. They brought us into the kingdom of God, and if it had not been for those two missionaries who left their homes . . . "

This was as far as he got. He saw the trap the bishop had laid for him, and with tears rolling down his cheeks he said, "Bishop, take him. I will see that he goes on a mission."

"And faith, hope, charity and love, with an eye single to the glory of God, qualify him for the work." (Doctrine and Covenants 4:5.) When we help Jesus in his great program of saving souls, we are incidentally saving our own.

Callings by True Authority

What is the strength of the Mormon position? I believe it is the gift of the Holy Ghost. This third member of the Godhead is to be the teacher of the Saints; the one who is to lead, guide, and direct in the paths of truth and righteousness; to give each of us a burning testimony; to set up a divine affinity, if you will, between God and man.

It has always interested me, because of the experiences of my own life, how we are called to positions through divine inspiration.

When I was living in Manti, Utah, many years ago, I was serving in our ward bishopric. One evening before stake conference, Elder Charles A. Callis and Rudger Clawson of the Council of the Twelve came down to reorganize the stake. A special meeting was held with the bishoprics and high council.

At about eleven o'clock the evening before conference, just before I dozed off to sleep, I heard someone tap on my window. It was my bishop, Alphonso Henry, and he said, "Leland, I've just come from a meeting of the visiting Brethren, and they have said that they will release me tomorrow and that they will put in a new bishop. They asked for recommendations, and I informed them that you are the one who should take my place."

I did not tell my wife anything about this message. I simply walked the floor all night, wondering how in the world I would ever carry on as bishop, since I was already the superintendent of our school system, with responsibility for all the schools in South Sanpete County.

At breakfast the next morning I was still wondering when I would be told of the changes to take place. Then, just before I was to leave for the first session of conference, the telephone rang. I turned white, and my wife asked me what the trouble was. I said, "Well, that's it, Blanche, that's it!"

"What is it?"

"That phone call. You will probably have an experience tonight you've never had in all your life before."

"What is that?"

I told her, "By tonight you will be living with the bishop of the Center Ward."

She threw up her hands and said, "Oh, no, Leland! You can't be bishop!"

"I can if the Lord puts me in there," I replied.

And of course she knew that I would accept the call, and she'd be the first one to back me up, because of her great faith.

Well, I answered the phone. President Lewis R. Anderson said, "The Brethren wish you to come out here as quickly as you can."

I said, "I'll be right out."

As I walked into President Anderson's home, there wasn't the usual greeting of handshaking. I just walked into the home and Elder Clawson came up to me and said, "Brother Anderson, the Lord wants you to be president of this stake."

I nearly went into shock. I said, "Brother Clawson, don't you mean be bishop of the Center Ward?"

"No," he said. "I don't mean bishop of the Center Ward. I mean president of the stake, and I'll give you exactly ten minutes to select your counselors."

"President, you select them," I said. "You have in mind other men in our stake who will gladly accept the call."

"No, my son," he replied. "It is not our right to suggest. It is your right to appoint and call your counselors."

I thought for a moment. And while I was thinking, Elder Callis took a piece of paper and pencil and wrote down two names. Then he folded the paper. He said, "These are the two men the Lord has just inspired me that you should call as your counselors."

I said, "Please hand it to me. I'll take them both."

"Oh, no," he said. "That's not the way it's done in the Church."

So I thought for a moment and also said a silent prayer. Then I said, "I'd like Edgar T. Reed, bishop of the Manti North Ward, for my first counselor, and President Ruel E. Christensen of Ephraim as my second counselor."

He handed me the paper, and on it he had written, "Edgar T. Reed, first counselor, and Ruel E. Christensen, second counselor."

I was told, "We'll call you brethren to the front just before the morning session ends, and you will give your acceptance speeches."

That was our call. I have often wondered why it happened as it did. But I know that God lives, and I know that he prompted the Brethren — at least as to whom I should select as my counselors.

"Scatterization of the Parts"

When I was on a mission in the deep South, I heard a story about a young boy who was on his way to Sunday School. As he walked down the country road, he suddenly fell to the ground in a convulsion. His parents tried to locate their family doctor but were unsuccessful. Finally they contacted an unknown country doctor who agreed to come and look at the boy.

He arrived within a few minutes and found the boy still under the influence of the spell. So he opened his medicine case and from it took some medicine and gave the boy a spoonful. It seemed to pull the boy's muscles together so that he was able to control his movements. Then the doctor took out another bottle of medicine and gave the boy a spoonful, and the boy pulled himself together and was normal again.

About that time the family's doctor arrived, and he asked the country doctor, "How did you diagnose this case?"

"Well, sir," was the reply, "as I saw this boy flopping around in the dirt, I thought he had what I call 'scatterization of the parts.' "

The family doctor asked, "What did you do for him?"

"I gave him a spoonful of alum."

"Alum? Good heavens, what was that for?"

"To pull all those parts together."

"Well, then what did you give him?"

"I gave him a spoonful of rosin."

"Rosin?"

"Yes."

"What on earth for?"

"To hold those parts together."

Some of our teachers develop "scatterization of the parts" every once in a while, especially when they're trying to discuss the Fall and the Atonement. I've seen many teachers almost fail through such "scatterization," not knowing how to proceed and why.

Often, in order to avoid this in our teaching, we need to outline the lesson in such a way that it's loaded with alum and rosin. The student must be able to find his way, not be left hanging out on a limb. Some things must be firm; they must be truth and must stand the test of ages. There must be points of reference to which the student can return and from which he can always find the same answer. In our teaching we must avoid "scatterization of the parts."

Personalizing Your Teaching

Never before do I recall such a concerted effort by our Church teachers to implant in the souls of the Saints the truths we live by and show how these truths may be incorporated into our lives. In this connection my uncle, Lewis Anderson, taught me a wonderful lesson, one that I've never forgotten, about doing good to those who do evil to us.

One day as we were taking a load of hay down the lane into the corral, we noticed three boys in my uncle's chicken coop stealing eggs. It happened that Uncle Lewis had many white leghorn chickens, from which he made a little money. At that time money was a little hard to come by — in fact, few people had any. All the stores had scrip, and you could buy things by selling or exchanging wheat, oats, and hay with the man who ran the store.

Across the road from my uncle was a ninety-year-old man named Kennykenick, who operated a little grocery store and candy shop. For one cent one could buy two big pieces of candy, and many of the boys would go out into their mothers' chicken coops and take an egg or two to go down and buy candy. Well, here were some boys doing this very thing — taking eggs from my uncle.

As he pulled into the corral, Uncle Lewis saw the boys quickly hide behind the door of the chicken coop. He handed me the lines and said, "Hold this team." Then he went down into the corral, through the barn, and entered the chicken coop by another way, a secret passage. As he stepped into the coop, he saw one boy holding a hat into which the other two had been putting eggs, going around to the nests and picking an egg here and one there. He watched them for a second, then coughed. And as they turned and saw him, they froze solid in their tracks.

The boys expected a fight — that was the proper way to settle things in that day. But my Uncle Lewis didn't do that. He started to go along the nests, picking up an egg here and an egg there and going over and putting them into the hat. He kept it up until the hat was full, while the boy holding it just stood there, awestruck.

The boys didn't know what to do. They couldn't run away, and they couldn't get out of the chicken coop. Then my uncle said, "Now boys, if you will come back again tomorrow, I will give you another hat full of eggs, because these chickens have a sweet habit of laying one every day." At that, he started for the door.

The boys looked at each other, then at Uncle Lewis, then walked over to the nests and began replacing the eggs. Then they walked out of the chicken coop and up the lane.

That night while we were eating supper, a knock came at the door and in walked the three boys. They wanted to talk to Uncle Lewis.

He took them into the parlor, and there they had a long talk. He taught them the importance of the commandment, "Thou shalt not steal," and told them the depths of evil that would come to them if they continued to try to get something for nothing. They agreed with him, and a couple of them shed a tear or two.

As they left, they each shook hands with Uncle Lewis, who said, "Boys, if you're ever in need of a little change, I'd be glad to give you work around here to do in my lot — weeding the garden or otherwise — so you can earn some spending money."

These boys, by the way, all grew up to be fine citizens in the community and leaders in the Church. Uncle Lewis had shown them the way; and this is one of the finest ways I know of to personalize your teaching.